Nature Recycles
How About You?

by Michelle Lord

illustrated by Cathy Morrison

The decorator sea urchin lives in the Atlantic Ocean. The water is warm, but he covers up. Urchin wears colorful algae, rocks, or coral. He wears ocean refuse like old oyster shells. These coverings protect him from rough waves and from the sun's strong rays. The decorations might even help the urchin hide from predators. He looks ready for a party dressed in his recycled green and pink outfit.

Urchin recycles.
How about you?

The hermit crab cannot grow his own shell. He finds a sea snail's shell in the sand. He makes it his new home. The shell protects his soft body from predators. When he outgrows it, he will search for a larger home.

Hermit crab helps keep the earth beautiful too. He cleans the shore by eating rotting ocean debris. The beach would be a mess without him.

Crab recycles.
How about you?

"*Tea-kettle. Tea-kettle,*" the Carolina wren sings. In April, the female lays five eggs in Dad's old boot. The wren and her mate gathered twigs, spider webs, leaves, trash, and snakeskin. They built a cozy nest from these discarded materials. They used feathers and dog hair too. This made a warm bed for their eggs.

Wren recycles.
How about you?

Yip. Yip. Yip. In the hot Sonoran Desert, an elf owl searches for a place to nest. Her yellow eyes spot an old woodpecker hole in the hundred-year-old saguaro cactus. She reuses this abandoned hole. This recycled hollow is a safe home for her and her three chicks.

Owl recycles.
How about you?

A veined octopus lives in the Indian Ocean. He explores the ocean floor. Octopus finds empty coconut halves. He carries the coconut halves for later use. *Poof!* When the octopus senses trouble, he claps the coconut together and hides inside.

Octopus recycles.
How about you?

Splash! Smash! Waves crash around the Galapagos Islands. Up in the branches, the woodpecker finch's short tongue cannot reach his food. This bird uses a discarded cactus spine. The spine was a perch, but now it is a tool that can be used again and again. He holds the tool in his beak. He plucks out a juicy grub. Dinnertime!

Finch recycles.
How about you?

The strong smell of manure fills the air. A shiny dung beetle rolls rhino poop into a ball. The beetle eats the waste of grass-eating animals. It uses the waste in its burrow to feed its hatchlings. The beetle reduces the amount of dung in grasslands. By returning the nutrients to the soil, this recycling process is good for the earth.

Beetle recycles.
How about you?

Sizzle. Scorch. A huge tower bakes on the hot savanna. Sand and dead plants are turned into a new nest by some mound-building termites. When they abandon their mound; snakes, birds, or mammals move in. These animals recycle the mound too. They use it as a shelter of their own.

Termites recycle.
How about you?

Water rushes down the stream. Here, a caddisfly larva builds a case around itself. Instead of brick or log walls, it recycles small pebbles, sand, or other discarded river items. Homemade glue sticks it all together. The larva's little stone house protects it from hungry trout. Larva helps keep the river clean too. It eats dead leaves and debris.

Larva recycles.
How about you?

Drip. Drip. Drop. Deep in the rainforest, a bromeliad plant fills with rain. The poison dart frog carries his babies on his back. He looks for a home for his tadpoles. He drops each tadpole into its own water-filled bromeliad leaf or even a Brazil nut pod tossed out by a blue and gold macaw. The tiny father feeds them until they grow into froglets. Frog reuses leaves and nut pods as cradles for his young.

Frog recycles.
How about you?

Buzzzz. Pesky flies nip at an Asian elephant's wrinkled hide. Her ears are not big enough to swis so many flies away. She grabs a banana leaf from the forest floor. *Swish-Swoosh.*

Asian elephant reuses the fallen leaf. She waves the flies away. Then she uses leaf in a new way—lunch. She devours it in a few bites!

Elephant recycles.
How about you?

Plants and animals need water to live. The sun heats rivers, lakes, and oceans. Water turns to vapor. The vapor cools and forms clouds. When clouds are full, we get precipitation: rain, sleet, or snow. Water fills rivers, lakes, and oceans once again. The earth recycles water over and over.

Earth recycles.
How about you?

Shuffle-Kerplunk. Shuffle-Kerplunk. I pick up trash along the river and around the park. I help keep turtles safe. They can get stuck in plastic soda holders and die.

I rest on the bench made of recycled plastic, like the bottles I collect.

I will take the plastic and aluminum to the recycling plant.

I recycle my clothes too. When I grow too big for my shirt, I use it as a rag to wash my bike!

I recycle.
How about you?

For Creative Minds

Why Animals Recycle

From the ocean floor to the dry desert, animals keep their habitats healthy by reducing, reusing, and recycling.

Some animals use plants or other items to build nests or shelter.

Other animals use bits and pieces of things to camouflage or protect themselves.

Some animals might even use items as tools to help them get food or make shelter.

Last, but not least, animals that eat dead plants and animals turn those things into nutrients for plants to grow, giving other animals food to eat.

Can you tell which animals recycle for nests or shelters, camouflage or protection, as tools, or as nutrients?

sea urchins

hermit crabs

Carolina wrens

Scientists think decorator urchins cover themselves with bits and pieces of shells or plants to protect themselves from the sun—like a sunscreen! The decorations may also protect them from other animals.

Hermit crabs have soft outer coverings (exoskeletons) so they reuse snail shells to protect themselves. When they outgrow one shell, they find a bigger one. They help keep our oceans clean by eating plants and animals that have died.

Both male and female Carolina wrens build nests using all kinds of recycled materials: tree bark, grass, leaves, hair, feathers, even plastic or string. They usually build the nests in tree holes but nests have been found in people's boots, old flowerpots, and even mailboxes!

elf owls   veined octopuses   woodpecker finches   dung beetles

Elf owls build their nests in abandoned woodpecker holes in trees and cacti.

Many octopuses use bottles or even cans as shelter. But the veined octopus carries pieces of clam or coconut shells. If scared, they'll tuck into the shell and pull it over them for protection.

Woodpecker finches use small twigs or cactus spines to pry insects (food) out of tree bark.

Dung beetles bury animal waste (feces) to lay their eggs. By digging, they loosen the soil and as the eggs hatch and eat the animal waste, they turn the waste into nutrients in the soil for plants to grow.

Termites recycle wood and plants into their nests. When they leave the nests, many other animals will move in and recycle the nest again!

Caddisfly larvae use plants, pebbles, sand, and even tiny shells to build protective shells for their pupae stage.

After dart frog tadpoles hatch, the fathers move the tadpoles to small wet "ponds" in nutshells, flower leaves, or even in old cans.

Asian elephants use their trunks to pull leaves off banana trees and fan themselves. They will also pick up sticks to scratch their backs.

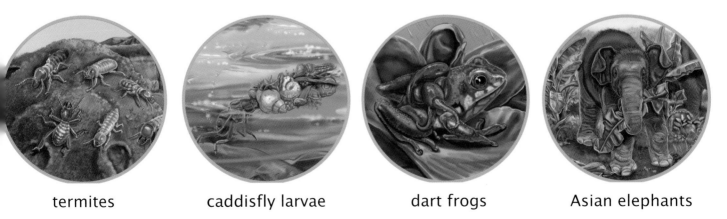

termites   caddisfly larvae   dart frogs   Asian elephants

Possible answers: nests or shelter: Carolina wrens, elf owls, veined octopus, dung beetles, termites, caddisfly larvae; camouflage or protection: decorator urchins, hermit crabs, dart frogs; tools: hermit crabs, veined octopus, woodpecker finches, Asian elephants; nutrients to soil: dung beetles

Where in the World? A Map Activity

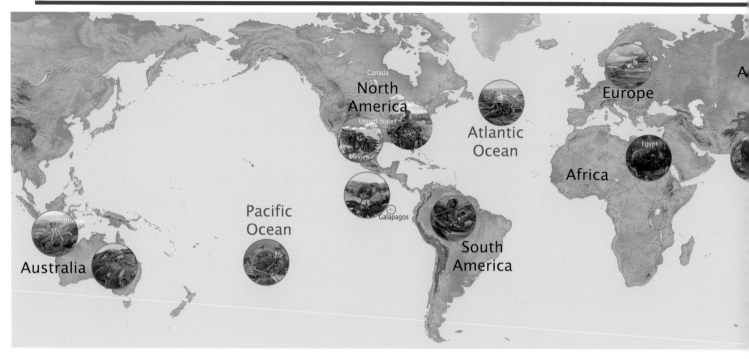

Find the animals on the map:

Decorator urchins live near the shore in shallow ocean water all over the world. Find the decorator urchin in the Pacific Ocean.

There are more than 500 different kinds of hermit crabs. A few live on land but most live in shallow ocean waters and estuaries. Find the hermit crab in the Atlantic Ocean.

Carolina wrens live in forests and areas with thick bushes in much of the eastern half of North America.

Elf owls are active at night and live in wooded and desert areas in Northern Mexico and the Southwest United States.

Veined octopuses live in sandy or muddy areas in the tropical waters around Australia and Indonesia.

Woodpecker finches live in wooded areas on the Galapagos Islands, in the Pacific Ocean off the coast of Ecuador, South America.

Dung beetles live in deserts, farmlands, forests, and grasslands on all continents except Antarctica. These insects were sacred to ancient Egyptians (in Northern Africa)

Termites live in a wide variety of land habitats on all continents except for Antarctica. The bandicoot living in the termite mound would only be found in Australia.

Caddisflies lay eggs in freshwater (streams, rivers, lakes and ponds) on all continents excep for Antarctica. Find the larvae in Europe.

Dart frogs live in tropical rainforests of Central and South America.

Asian elephants live in Southeast Asia.

Reduce, Reuse, and Recycle: True or False?

Reduce means to buy or use less of something. What can you do to reduce waste?
- Turn off lights when leaving a room.
- Take reusable bags to the store instead of using bags from the store.

Reuse is to use something more than once. What can you and your family reuse?
- Reuse cardboard boxes to build a fort.
- Reuse plastic sandwich baggies.

Recycle is to make a new item from something that has been used before. Many items can be recycled: paper, plastic, metal, glass, electronics and more! Look for products made from recycled items. Glass can be turned into sports turf or countertops. Plastic is made into carpet, fleece jackets, or outdoor furniture. What are some things you and your family could recycle each week?
- Recycle newspaper into gift-wrap.
- Recycle jelly jars into drinking glasses.
- Recycle empty plastic food containers into containers for toys.

Which of the following statements are true and which are false?

1. A yard sale is a good place to look for something you need instead of buying something new.

2. You should not turn off the water while brushing your teeth or washing your hands.

3. Drive places instead of riding a bike because oil and gasoline are renewable resources.

4. Reduce waste by donating your outgrown clothes instead of throwing out and adding trash to crowded landfills.

5. Never use bath towels more than once or wear clothes more than one time before washing.

6. Paper napkins are much better for the environment than cloth napkins.

7. An average shower uses 5-10 gallons every minute.

8. Polyester is a good fabric to choose for your clothing.

9. Vermicomposting is the process of using worms to turn food waste into plant fertilizer.

10. Plastic grocery bags pollute the environment, harm animals, and take hundreds of years to decompose.

Answers: 1) True; 2) False: You can save 8 gallons of water each day by turning off the water while brushing your teeth! Turn off the water while soaping your hands to save even more water. 3) False: Try to walk or ride a bike when you can. Oil and gas are non-renewable resources. 4) True; 5) False: Try to reuse clothing and towels if they are not dirty. This saves water and your clothes will last longer. Hang clothes to dry rather than using excess energy with the dryer. 6) False: Cloth napkins can be used over and over again. Paper napkins add to landfills if not recycled. 7) True; 8) False: Polyester is made from petroleum, a non-renewable resource. 9) True; 10) True

For my husband Marshall, an avid recycler. Thanks for making my world a better place!—ML
To my great nephew, Oliver Grier Luke. Oliver recycles. How about you?—CM
Thanks to Jaclyn Stallard, Manager of Education Programs at Project Learning Tree (www.plt.org) for verifying the accura
of the information in this book.

Library of Congress Cataloging-in-Publication Data

Lord, Michelle.
 Nature recycles : how about you? / by Michelle Lord ; illustrated by Cathy Morrison.
    p. cm.
 ISBN 978-1-60718-615-1 (english hardcover) -- ISBN 978-1-60718-711-0 (spanish hardcover) -- ISBN 978-1-60718-627-4
(english pbk.) -- ISBN 978-1-62855-349-9 (spanish pbk.) -- ISBN 978-1-60718-639-7 (english ebook (downloadable)) -- ISB
978-1-60718-651-9 (spanish ebook (downloadable)) -- ISBN 978-1-60718-663-2 (interactive english/spanish ebook (web-
based)) 1. Recycling (Waste, etc.)--Juvenile literature. 2. Environmentalism--Juvenile literature. I. Morrison, Cathy, ill. II.
Title.
 TD794.5.L66 2013
 363.72'82--dc23

                         2012031348

Nature Recycles—How About You?: Original Title in English
La naturaleza recicla—¿Lo haces tú?: Spanish Title

Lexile® Level: 600L   key phrases for educators: recycling, conservation, geography, repeating phrases

Manufactured in China, December 2017
This product conforms to CPSIA 2008
Third Printing

Arbordale Publishing
formerly Sylvan Dell Publishing
Mt. Pleasant, SC 29464
www.ArbordalePublishing.com